in the swim

poems and paintings by

Douglas Florian

voyager books

harcourt, inc.

SAN DIEGO · NEW YORK · LONDON

www.harcourt.com

First Voyager Books edition 2001
Voyager Books is a trademark of Harcourt, Inc.,
registered in the United States of America and other jurisdictions.

The Library of Congress has cataloged the hardcover edition as follows:
Florian, Douglas.
In the swim: poems and paintings/by Douglas Florian.
p.   cm.
Summary: A collection of humorous poems about such underwater creatures
as the starfish, piranha, and clam.
1. Marine fauna—Juvenile poetry.   2. Children's poetry, American.
[1. Marine animals—Poetry.   2. Humorous poetry.   3. American poetry.]   I. Title.
PS3556.L589I5   1997
811'.54—dc20   95-52616
ISBN 0-15-201307-5
ISBN 0-15-202437-9 pb

A C E G H F D B

The illustrations in this book were done in watercolor on rough French watercolor paper.
The display type was set in Belwe Light.
The text type was set in Sabon.
Color separations by Classicscan Pte. Ltd., Singapore
Printed and bound by Tien Wah Press, Singapore
This book was printed on Arctic matte paper.
Production supervision by Sandra Grebenar and Pascha Gerlinger
Designed by Kaelin Chappell

Contents

The Catfish

I cannot purr.
I don't have fur
Or claws or paws.
Don't sleep in drawers.
I don't chase mice.
Let that suffice.
I am a fish.
I have no wish
To be a cat.
That's that!

Could do with legs!

Just think what we

Our pearly eggs.

Upstream we spawn

We somersault!

We vault!

We jump!

Our leaps astound!

We bound!

We spring!

The Salmon

The Piranhas

It's widely known
That grown piranhas
Are long on teeth
But short on manners.

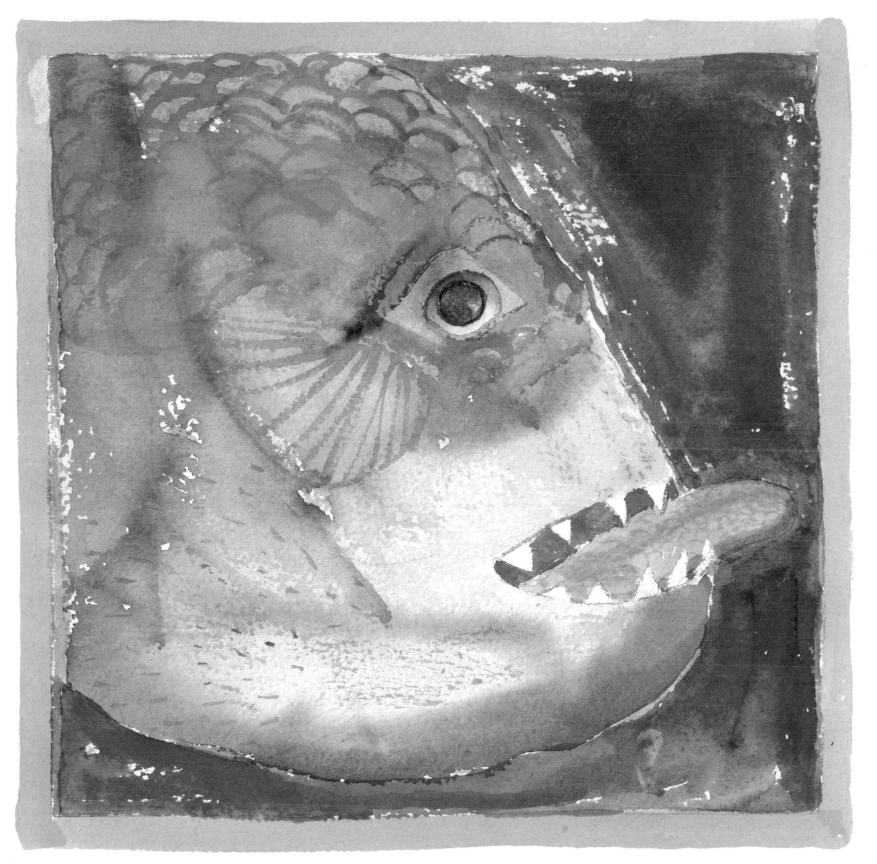

The Eel

Some people make
A big mistake:
They try to take
Me for a snake.
A snake is not
So smooth or slimy.
My gills and fins
Identify me.
Here's the secret
Of the century:
An eel is a fish—
It's eel-ementary!

The Sawfish

You'll see a saw

Upon my jaw,

But I can't cut

A two-by-four,

Or build a bed,

Or frame a door.

My splendid saw's

For goring fishes—

I eat them raw

And don't do dishes.

14

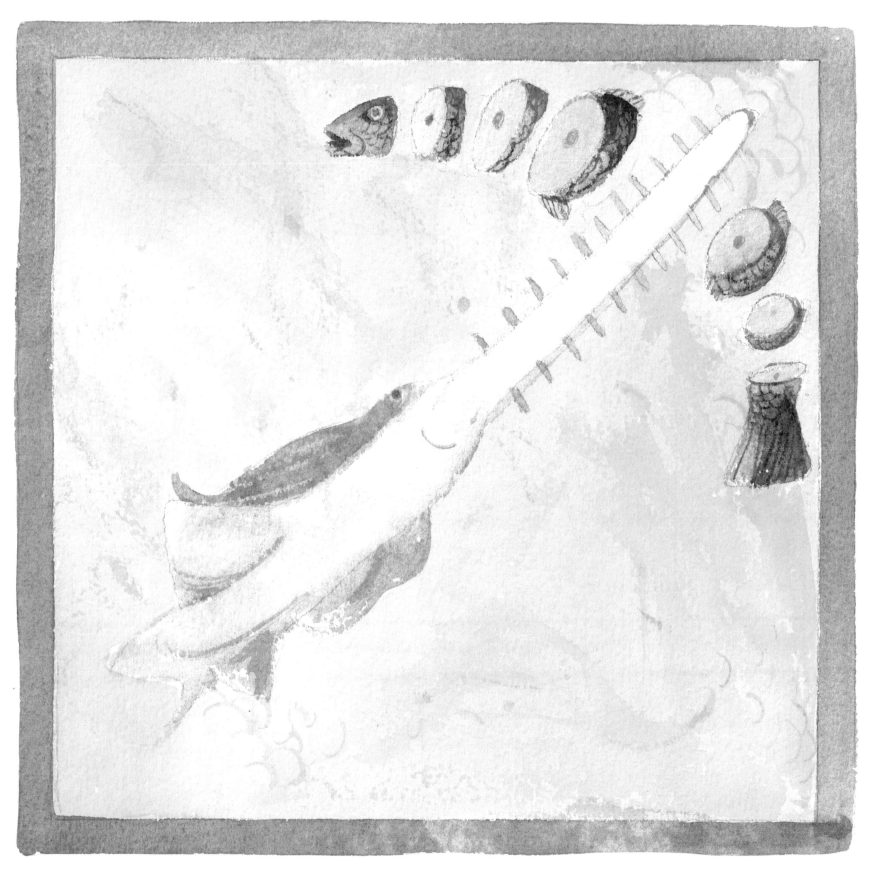

15

The Sea Horse

You have
No hooves.
You have no hair.
You don't eat oats.
You don't breathe air.
You hatch from eggs.
You cannot race.
(You have no legs
With which to chase.)
You're not a colt
Nor mare
Nor filly.
You're called a horse.
I call that silly.

The Whale

W i d e as a wall
And just as tall.
A wall with a tail.
A ship.
A sail.
A wharf.
A W H A L E.

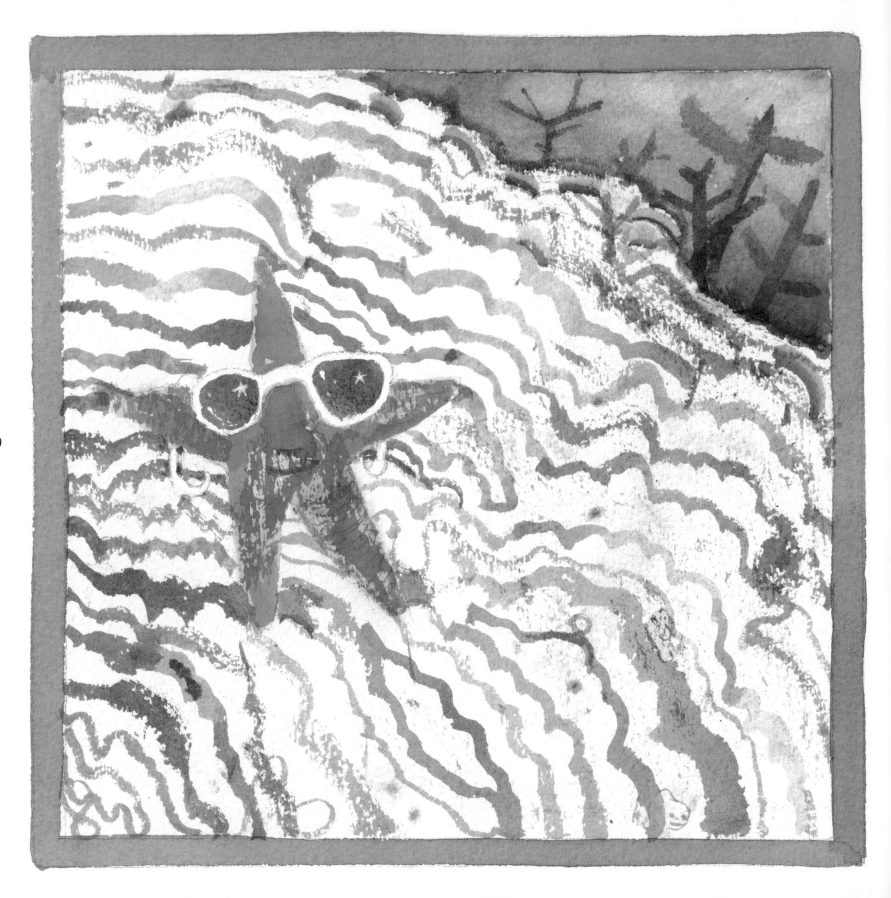

The Starfish

Although it seems
That I'm all arms,
Some other organs
Give me charm.
I have a mouth
With which to feed.
A tiny stomach
Is all I need.
And though it's true
I have no brain,
I'm still a *star*—
I can't complain.

The Ray

Grand and gray
The regal ray
Slyly g l i d e s
Upon its prey.
It almost flies
On weightless wings.
Its whiplike tail
With poison stings.
All creatures near
This royal ray
Retreat in fear:
Make way!
Make way!

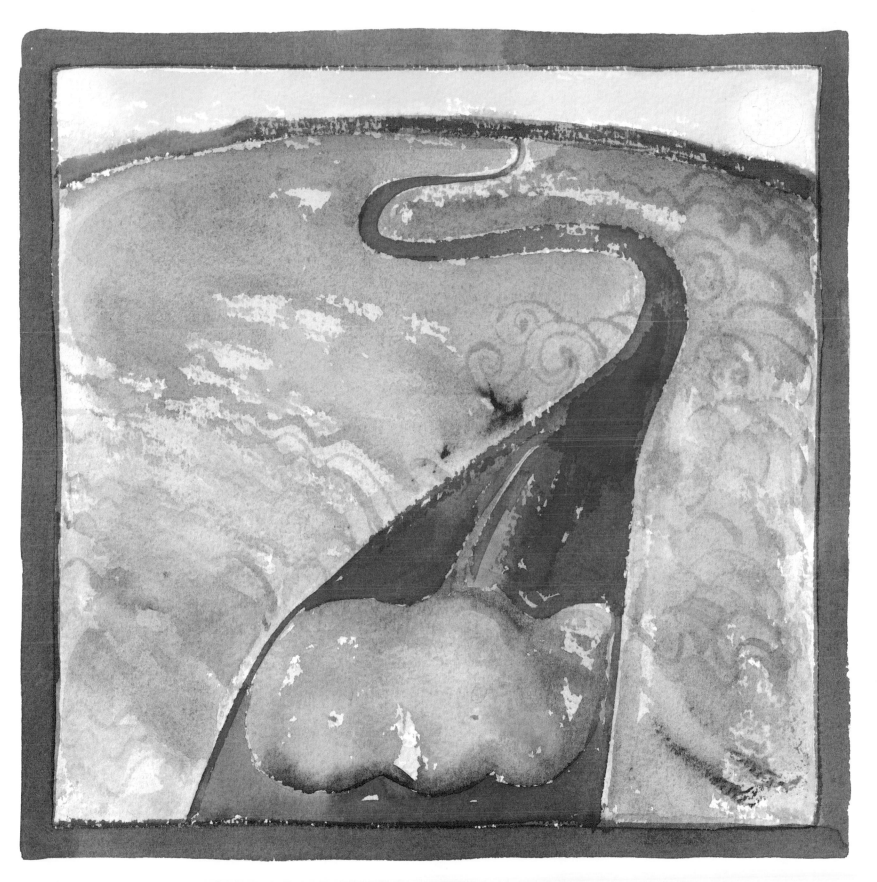

The Flounders

Flat as a pancake
Flat as a crepe
Flounders are flat
As a prairie in shape.
While waiting on
Their smooth white side
Below the sand
For food they hide,
Awaiting shrimp
And smaller fishes,
These flattish, mattish
Living dishes.

The Sharks

Sharks can park
Wherever they wish.
They do not fear
The other fish.
Sharks can swim
Wherever they please.
On this each other
Fish agrees.

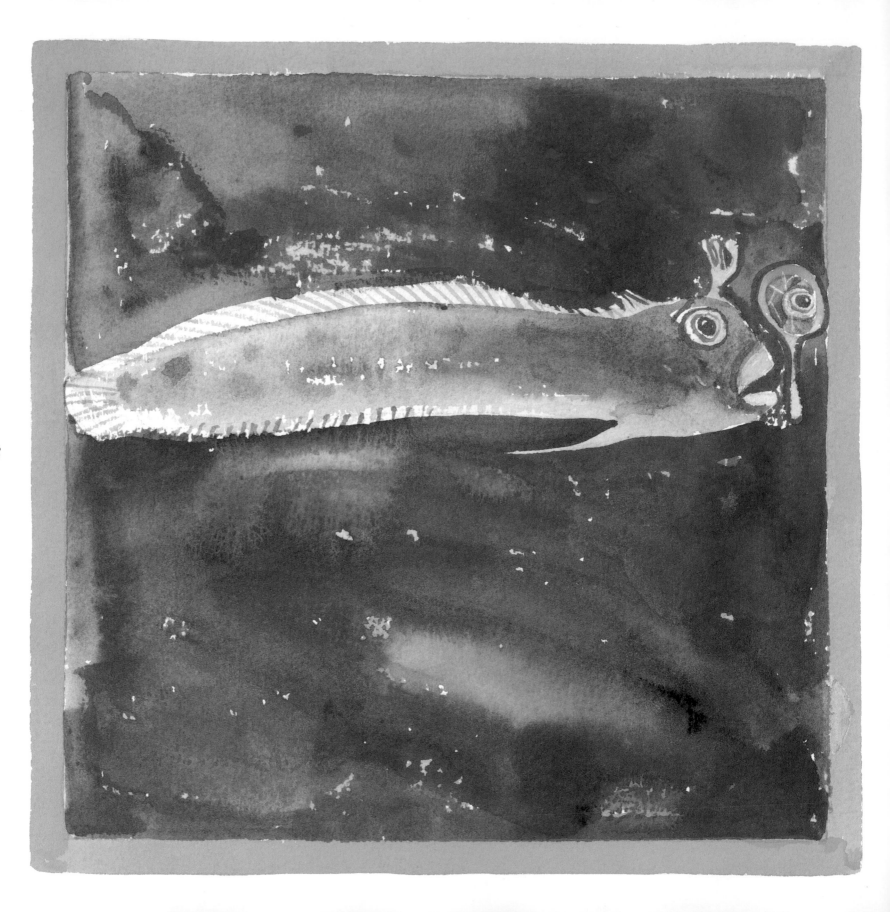

The Blenny

There are uglier fish than a blenny—

But not many.

The Flying Fish

We don't wish to brag or boast
But we can fly along the coast.
We don't want to rant or rave
But we can soar above a wave.
Side by side we glide and skim—
And by the way, we also swim!

The Clam

They say, "As happy as a clam,"
But would **you** like to have to cram
Your body deep inside a shell?
And furthermore: I think clams smell.

The Anglerfish

Lurking on the ocean floor
There works a crafty carnivore.
The anglerfish has set a trap
With its dangling, fleshy flap,
Complete with fishing pole and bait,
And all it has to do is wait
For some poor fish to take the lure
And make the ocean one fish fewer.

The Skates

The skinny skates are flat as plates.
They feed on small invertebrates
They find upon the ocean floor
Then skate along to find some more.

The Manatee

The manatee is not a man.
It's heavy as a minivan.
It has a bristly, big mustache,
And paddle tail to make a splash.
The manatee does not take tea.
It swallows plants beneath the sea.
It eats so much that it may seem
At times to be a manateam.

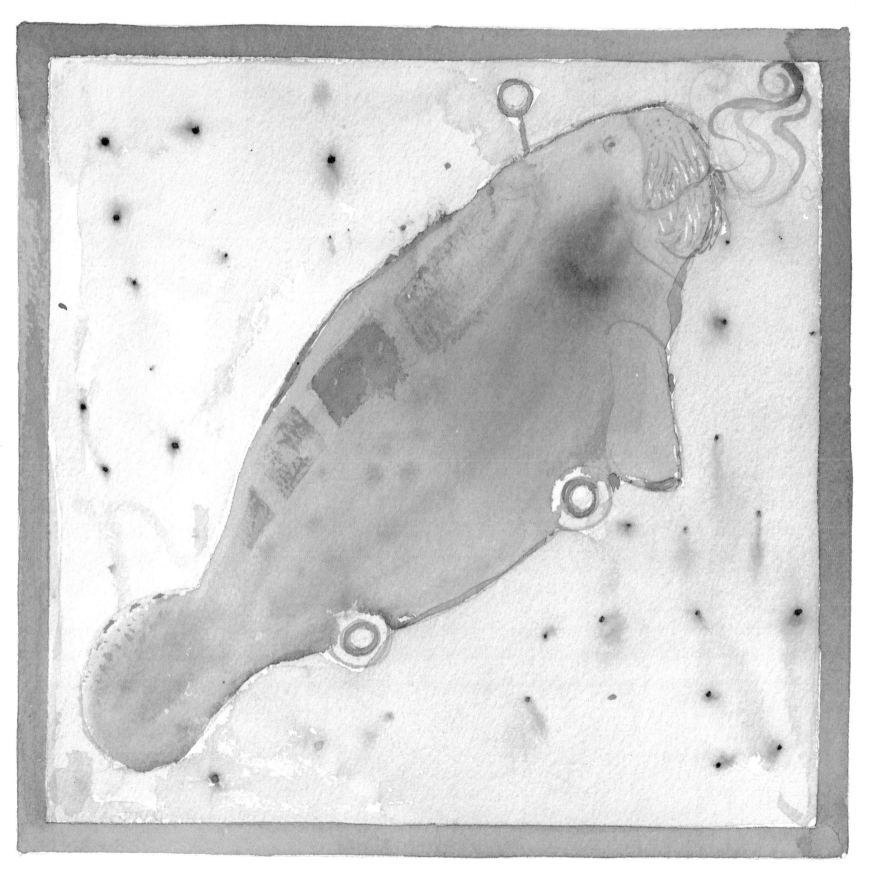

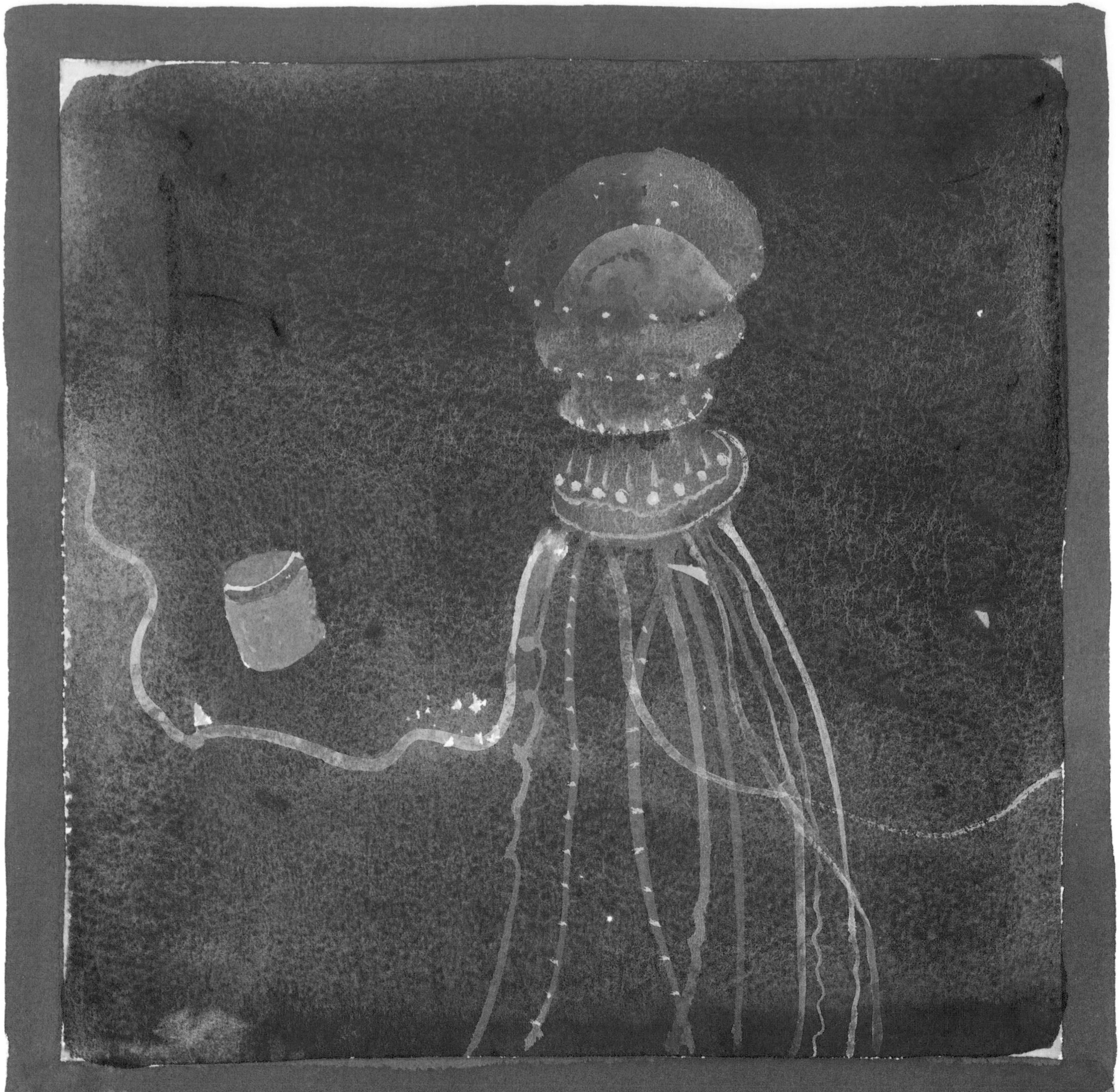

The Jellyfish

Thin
As a drape
Umbrella shaped,
It gently glides
Through the seascape.
Though small in size
And with no eyes
Its tentacles can paralyze.
In sporty spurts
It loves to flutter
In its vain search
For peanut
Butter.

The Oysters

Did you know the ocean's oysters
Sometimes change from girls to boysters?
Then the boys change back to girls.
(Are the girls the ones with pearls?)

The Rainbow Trout

So suave!
So chic!
So magnifique!
To sport a rainbow
On your cheek!
And down your flank!
So swell!
So swank!
Divine!
Delish!

Too bad you're a fish.

The Tetra

The itty-bitty, pretty tetra
Is small, minute, petite, et cetra.

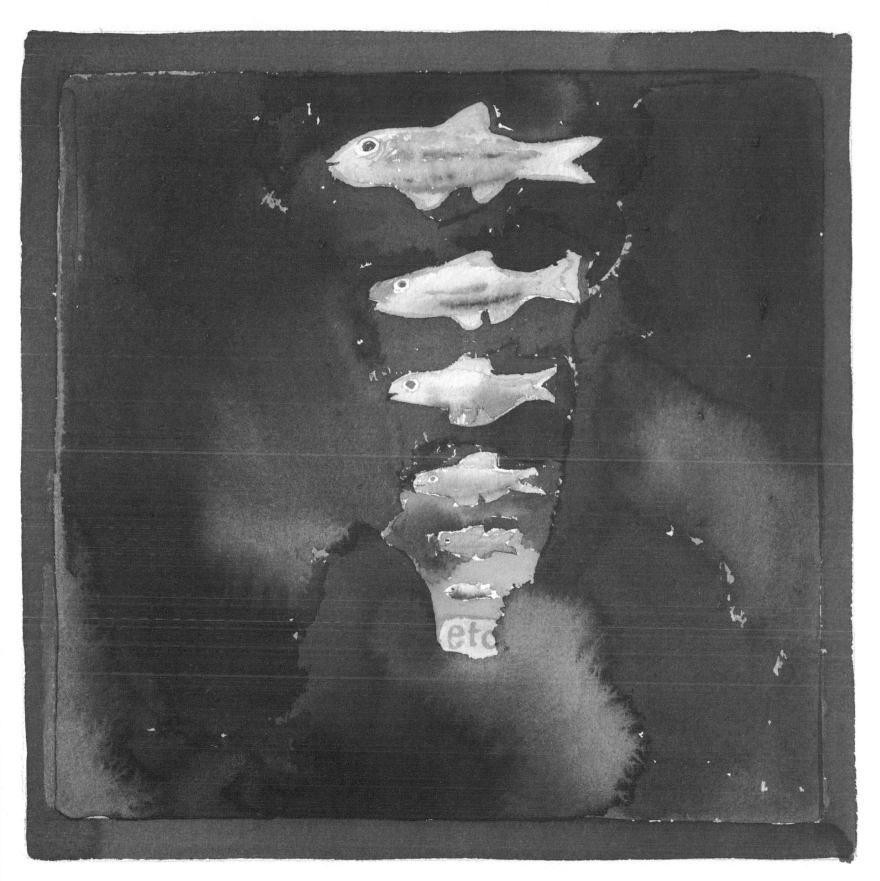

Companion books by Douglas Florian:

beast feast

★"Florian's distinctive, full-page watercolors are as playful as his verse."
—*Publishers Weekly* (starred review)

on the wing

"Nonfiction and humor don't always fit comfortably together, but in this
book they become a delightful whole."—*Kirkus Reviews*

insectlopedia

★"There are other books of poetry about insects...but none match *Insectlopedia*."
—*School Library Journal* (starred review)

mammalabilia

"A witty array...This is a worthy addition to Florian's pixilated
poetic stable of natural history."—*The Bulletin*

And don't miss Douglas Florian's newest collection...

lizards, frogs, and polliwogs